This igloo book belongs to:

....

igloobooks

Published in 2019
by Igloo Books Ltd
Cottage Farm
Sywell
NN6 0BJ
www.igloobooks.com

GOL002 0419
2 4 6 8 10 9 7 5 3 1
ISBN 978-1-78670-915-8

Written by Stephanie Moss
Illustrated by Melanie Mitchell

Designed by Jason Shortland
Edited by Hannah Cather

Printed and manufactured in China

I Want To Be Like YOU

Written by
Stephanie Moss

Illustrated by
Melanie Mitchell

igloobooks

Little Lion loved his friends. He thought they were the best!
He copied everything they did... but no one was impressed.

In fact, the baby animals were getting quite annoyed.
Little Lion was a friend that they were starting to avoid.

"Woo-hoo!" he would cry, as he tried swinging from tree to tree.
"I'm exactly like you, Monkey. Everybody, look at me!"

But Monkey replied crossly,
"Little Lion, don't do that.
Swinging is just for monkeys.
Don't be such a copycat."

His friends explained that doing your own thing isn't so bad.
But Little Lion didn't want to, then he started to feel sad.

"Being a lion is great!" they cried.
"Just be yourself, instead."

"But I want to be like you!"
poor Little Lion said.

So he stood tall like Giraffe and stomped like Elephant in her herd.

He pretended he had wings
and tried to flap them like a bird!

He tried to swim with Crocodile...

... and slither on the ground with Snake.

Until, one day, Little Lion made a very big mistake.

He tried to balance on one leg, just like flamingos do.
But he wobbled and fell in... then the flamingos all did, too!

Little Lion ran away.
"My friends were right all along.
I won't copy them again.
How could I have been so wrong?"

At first, his friends all cried, **"He's stopped at last. Hip-hip-hooray!"**

But soon they all missed him and hoped he would come back and play.

So, they planned a fancy dress party.
The best costume would win!

"Are you coming, Little Lion?"
asked Crocodile, with a grin.

"They've forgiven me," he said, "for what I did before.
I'll show them that I've changed. I won't copy any more."

He thought hard about the party to make sure that he'd stand out.
Then he gathered his supplies and spread them all about.

"I've got it!" he cried.
"I'll make a mane that I can wear.
It will look so good that
all my friends will stop and stare."

Little Lion set to work and soon his masterpiece was done.
Then, the jungle party started. Everyone was having fun!

At first he felt so nervous,
as he tiptoed through the crowd.

Then he saw his reflection
and he stood up tall and proud.

"Great costume, Little Lion," they said.
"You should win first prize!"

It felt so good to be himself, much to his surprise.

"We know you copy us to show the love that's in your heart,
but you should always be yourself, so you can stand apart."

Little Lion smiled and partied with his friends all night.
They each behaved just like themselves... and that felt just right!